The Parable of Rust

The Parable of Rust is a work of archetypical fiction. While some real places and persons are referenced, the names, characters, and incidents depicted either are products of the author's imagination or are used fictitiously. Any resemblance of these to actual events or locales or persons, living or dead, is purely coincidental and wholly the reader's subjective association.

ISBN: 978-1-7368877-1-4

Published by Ferrox Fiction

www.ferroxfiction.com

For her, who taught me

all possess a book within,

with hers so called home

Contents

The Parable of Rust

Prologue

The city of Rust is a Midwestern (post-)industrial town. Its boom and bust follows the lifecycle of the widget factory at its economic heart. A town of respectable size due to its Great Lakes access, Rust hit its prime when the interstate highway system placed it at the nexus of road, rail, and lake transportation networks and ideally suited for widget manufacturing. It collapsed when the forty year thread of useful economic life the fates of industrial economics dispense to major capital investments ran out. It is presently undergoing a modest recovery.

Behind that description is of course a human story.

Neu Röst was originally settled in the 1840s by Saxon emigres under the leadership of Ludwig von Röst. Ludwig discovered his *Anglo*-Saxon neighbors unable to properly pronounce the German long-O sound and capitulated to Anglicization as Lewis Rust. In an act of mild petulance he decreed that if the town's name was to be anglicized as well it was no longer *new* anything.

Nearly all the Midwest was surveyed by capable professionals; Rust existed outside the area so circumscribed. In fact, it literally existed outside the areas circumscribed by state borders as the Midwest was admitted to the union. The 1850s did not feature effective dispute resolution. The Southerners were not about to give the Yankees two senators in exchange for nothing, and the Free-Soilers were not about to countenance further westward expansion of the peculiar institution just to remedy minor incompetence. Rust itself was not going to settle for conglomeration into another state having had its hopes raised so high.

During the war, Rust threatened to declare independence and join the empire on the other side of the lakes. The purpose of the senators was moot, as *that* question was now being settled by force of arms. For that same reason, the Union could not afford a breach with the Commonwealth. No one *really* wanted to carve out *another* semi-invented new state, especially one lacking the size and strategic value of West Virginia. The whole secession business was out of the bag, but the entire problem derived from Rust never acceding as a state in the first place. Therefore no terrible precedent was set by granting Rust its independence, with a lopsided treaty requiring it to mirror most of the US's laws and strictly circumscribing (no mistakes this time) its foreign policy.

Rust was to be… a little bit different.

As iron sharpens iron, so one person sharpens another

Proverbs 27:17

The Parable of Rust

The roar of the twenties was the sound of blast furnaces. Norman Selbsteiger was not the quiet type. Rather than split the farm with his elder brother he launched a Great Lakes shipping company. He began with the family's produce but found his real niche feeding the furnaces of the great freshwater industrial colossi. What boosted Norman from bootstrap to baron was the war.

Rust existed in a gray zone at the edge of Washington's formal neutrality. American neutrality was limited by the cash & carry system, but Rust was too inconsequential to provoke a fight. The soon-to-be Allies could launder aid to the House of Windsor through Rust, provided Rustan-flagged vessels shipped the munitions to Windsor, ON, and a Potemkin factory permitted the pretense they were of Rustan manufacture. Selbsteiger Shipping could supply the former immediately and the latter in short order.

The "factory" needed only exist until Rust could manufacture a pretext to PNG the German Ambassador, who produced the requisite raw material like an open-pit mine. The Third Reich maintained previous

German governments' tradition of posting an ambassador. Ostensibly honoring distant kinship, its real purpose was to exile politely people of parentage too prominent to punish. Rust tolerated the indignity because the spending habits of such people made the system de facto state aid, augmented in the 30s by the expense accounts of the G-men dispatched to keep tabs on Herr Ambassador.

Their dispatches produced zero intelligence, but their boss was not one to forego lurid gossip: the Nazi respected social boundaries in the manner his compatriots respected national ones. The reports recorded which ladies in the social register resisted (nearly all) and appeased (a scandalous few) his intoxicated advances. An especially offensive such advance in the spring of 1940 towards the 17-year old Miss Louisa Rust (decisively repulsed) scandalized Rust and justified booting him. No replacement returned; intervening events focused attention elsewhere. Norman had intended to make the nominal factory real, but the absence of anyone to fool mooted the issue, and the site operated for the remainder of the war as a depot.

The young Norman Selbsteiger, Jr. served in the war, where he acquired the nickname "Selby" but never saw combat; the Allies deemed his logistical talent far too valuable to place anywhere near gunfire. Miss Louisa had a thing for smart, handsome men in uniform who were also heir-apparent to the most successful business in the city-state.

The couple wed upon Selby's demobilization, and Norman Jr. joined Norman Sr. at Selbsteiger & Son Shipping. By the end of the 50s Jr. was effectively running the whole business, with Sr. involved only for major, strategic decisions.

Such a decision point came in the mid-60s. The Selbsteigers were no dummies: *Pere et fils* were of one mind that the under-construction interstate highway system would sink their shipping business. The formal economic delineation of "network externalities" was still twenty years into the future (in any event neither Selbsteiger had ever sat in a lecture hall), but nonetheless they understood it exactly. Although the terminology is not what they would have used, they knew Rust *absolutely had to* have a node on this network, and Selbsteiger & Son needed a new business to capture a piece of that externality.

Getting connected was easy. Louisa's extended family in Rust's Assembly of Councilmen happily championed the idea independently of any Selbsteiger interests. A consensus in the Assembly formed shortly after a quorum-worth of councilmen acquired real estate on the landward edge of town. The Rustan delegation's insistence on the specifics of the right-of-way puzzled the DOT consulting engineers, but Washington agreed to foot the construction bill in exchange for updates to Rust's legal—and now regulatory—harmonization treaty, which breezed through the Senate.

Finding a new business turned out to be a bear. Integrating trucking into the existing shipping business seemed the obvious route, but Selby discovered it was nearly impossible for *Americans* to get a certificate of public convenience and necessity from the Interstate Commerce Commission, much less technical foreigners. Washington's attitude towards favors for Rustans had soured. A mutually unforeseen consequence of ratifying a treaty in the mid-60s highlighting Rust's technical foreignness and reaffirming mutual freedom of movement was suddenly becoming congenial to a certain category of American averse to military service. The attraction was entirely unrequited. Rust's expulsion attempts were foiled by the litigious Americans' frustratingly correct argument that Rust had no legal basis to do so.

Rust could have, had it wished, put the hammer down over the trucking issue. Rust's independence had left it out of the National Master Freight Agreement, and the Treaty permitted duplication of regulatory agencies provided identical hard rules. Creating a parallel ICC was a live option. A spree of vandalism and a visit from a pair of out-of-town gentlemen sporting pinky rings convinced Selby that avenue was a dark alley best avoided. All Selby acquired from his trucking tribulations was a burning hatred of unions.

The solution came out of the deep, deep blue from an old wartime logistics colleague. After the war, Jacob Katz had found his services valued too highly by the incipient military-industrial complex to escape its orbit until the beginning of the space program. This really only got him to high-atmosphere orbit. He managed the Wave-Infrared Device to Get Electronic Telemetry subproject (engineers produce some groaners) resulting from the realization that Gemini missions operated at durations and speeds where time-dilation was potentially nontrivial. Katz's mother back in Queens somehow knew that smart Richard boy from couple blocks over had managed to get patents *in his own name* working for the government out in the desert somewhere and had browbeaten Katz into doing the same.

Katz was ready for a boost phase to reach true escape velocity from the MIC. His employer (which had grown out of the Laboratory Annex of a sprawling Potomac Basin DoD research facility and now bore the boring corporate name of LABANCO) had for no clear reason passed him over a *second* time for promotion into its executive ranks. He was also ready to leave the Potomac Basin after a brusque rejection from the Ashmont Birchford CC. With cost-plus contracting, blank-check R&D budgets, stringent weight & amperage constraints, and an anticipated market size of 20, the unit cost of the WIDGET was as astronomical as its original purpose. Liberated from these limitations, Katz was certain WIDGETs could become a mass-produced consumer product and put a little piece of space-age sexiness into every two-car garage in America. He called up his old war buddy Selby to make his pitch.

The site was the obvious one: the old wartime depot had become a warehouse for Selbsteiger & Son. It had excellent road access to the port and a rail link courtesy of Uncle Sam and Her (then, His) Britannic Majesty's Governor-General. These provided Selby with powerful negotiating leverage with which he secured very competitive freight rates for the supply chain. Having learned with whom he was dealing from his previous failure, he protected said leverage this time with some well-compensated off-duty Murphys & O'Malleys who were positively *eager* to ensure no greasy vandals committed any property crimes in Rust. After two years of fine-tuning to get the widget to commercial readiness and a third to get the factory built, The Widget Company of Rust was open for business.

Gold

The early years of the factory were spectacularly successful, so much so that the Selbsteigers & Katz drew up plans to expand. The holdup was the union, or rather its indeterminate existence. The workers had certainly formed one; Selby refused to recognize it as a negotiating partner. The standoff had not yet resulted in a strike because the union's superposition was a consequence of legal uncertainty: it was not clear from the Highway Treaty which provisions of US labor law applied to Rust. The interference collapsed in mid-1975 when the US Ambassador observed the state of affairs and informed Rust its persistence would indeed violate the treaty in the eyes of Washington.

To resolve the impasse, Selby finally deigned to meet with the union president, a man by the name of Andy McKay. McKay had dropped out of school in Eastern Kentucky, hitch-hiked his way to Detroit during the prewar re-armament period, and found a gig driving trucks for the local 299. An incident of which he refused to ever speak had forced him out of the motor city and given him a bum knee that prevented him from enlisting (for which his family never forgave him).

He had bounced around the Midwest, limited by the knee to driving trucks. Every few years he had been let go and cryptically informed by his super that it "wasn't safe" for him there anymore. Rust was one of the few places left for him to give it a go. McKay's working days were nearly done, but he had found commanding respect among his fellow ex-Kentuckians, who made him their leader.

The Kentucky expatriates had immigrated *en masse* upon discovering the network effects of the interstate highway system included well-paying factory jobs within a day's drive of their ancestral homeland. At first they were more accurately described as guest workers who would actually undertake this commute every Friday and Sunday and rent accommodations by the week and, disconcertingly, sometimes by the hour. They had increasingly become permanent residents, a development native Rustans welcomed: permanent residency meant co-resident wives. Rustans were not eager to host *another* motley assemblage of young men unrestrained by a better half, and the wives were much more effective than the Rust PD at controlling the level of public intoxication, prostitution, and casual violence. Rust instituted the unique naturalization policy of issuing citizenship to the wives first to give them leverage and only later to the husbands once deemed adequately domesticated for civil society.

The preliminaries for Selby and McKay's meeting indicated the depth of mutual distrust. It was to be held at Metzger's, Rust's best (well, only) steakhouse. Labor and management spent the afternoon scouring the restaurant for recording devices and/or explosives and monitoring each other's searches. The restaurant was to be entirely empty except for Selby, McKay, and two trusted associates apiece who were to witness events and frisk the skeleton crew of wait staff. The associates were to supposed to remain within visual sight of but out of earshot from the conversation. The snippet they did catch they couldn't quite follow.

"It takes a lot of nerve for you guys to send a trucker from Detroit. The likes of you have caused me a lot of pain and suffering."

"Don't talk to me about pain and suffering until they've made you limp for thirty-five years. I ain't who you take me for."

"Fair enough. Sounds like it's not just your knee that still hurts."

"Where I come from forgiveness don't come cheap. Four years might be enough for Dick. Not for me."

"So that's what you've still got a 7-year old bumper sticker for a dead man in a different country."

"Gotta be careful saying it, but Bobby getting assassinated was a bigger loss than Jack."

"Imagine that, an old trucker and an old shipping baron seeing eye-to-eye on something."

"You used to be in shipping?"

"Technically still am. One carrier left to liquidate. Lake traffic is not what it used to be."

"So I'm not the only one here who knows my way around Detroit's docks. I bet we've got some old mutual acquaintances."

"You asked me not to speak of my pain and suffering. Those greaseballs are PNG in my town for a reason."

"And I'm glad that's true. It's how I wound up here. But I think there's a way for all of us to get squared up. They don't want the bad old days back either."

"I'm listening."

"My old business is the landward side of ports. I can get cargo in. Your old business is the maritime side. You can get cargo out. I believe that's what folks call 'complimentary.'"

"Mr. McKay, I believe you and I will be able to do business."

The dinner ended up taking three full hours but concluded with a handshake. The tired and anxious workers had camped out in the parking lot, prompting the erection of a police barricade Just In Case. McKay and Selby emerged, announced a deal, and embraced. Jubilation ensued. Neither side got exactly what they wanted but such is the nature of negotiated agreement. The critical victory was the establishment of peace. Going forward management and labor could trust each other to deal in good faith. Both had too much to lose from a breach.

Selby and McKay established a tradition to re-enact the dinner every year on July 30th, which was odd because the increasingly legendary parley had actually occurred on the 17th, the labor agreement had been signed a week later, and the expansion groundbreaking had been on August 2nd. Correction: the *ceremony* had been on the 2nd. Someone had jumped the gun and poured the first of the foundation slabs during the previous night. It was the only time anyone recalled Andrew McKay giving a genuine grin. His chronic knee pain, smoker's cough, and general gruffness had produced a perma-grimace everyone knew him by, but that day he wore a satisfied smile.

The traditions of The Peace Dinner grew elaborate over the years. To be selected as one of the two associates tasked with the ritual frisking of Metzger's wait staff became a great honor and a sign of future advancement. In a nod to the ethno-cultural differences no one liked to talk about but which marked the Widget Company of Rust and increasingly the city as a whole, gifts were exchanged. From management to labor: pilsner from the old country (sometimes just from Milwaukee). From labor to management: a cask of bourbon from *their* old country. Pageantry aside, Selby & Andy always ensured they had at least an hour in private to discuss real business, which averted many an incipient problem.

About those ethno-cultural differences: Rust in its heyday most certainly had a class structure. Kids figured out by about twelve that one could predict by surname who had a VP title in their future and whose corporate ladder reached only as high as "foreman." Despite that, Schmidts and Smiths still shared the same little league, schools, and bowling tournaments. They were as often as not next-street if not next-door neighbors. The edges were sharper amongst the women, but the details of that were completely inscrutable to Rust's menfolk.

The schools were where order was really kept. Anyone on the VP life track who got snotty about it could be rebuked with a pointed hit at football practice or in egregious cases a black eye. At home his mother would fuss that he shouldn't be getting into fights at all but that it was still terrible what that boy did. The real lesson came after dinner, alone with his father.

"Why'd you lose the fight?"

"Idunno, because I wasn't expecting it?"

"Why on earth not?"

"What do you mean? *He* started it!"

"That's where you're wrong. *He* only threw the first punch. *You* started the fight. I talked to Coach Herrmann. I know what you said."

"*So what?* His dumb ass *is* going to work for me some day, just like his dumbass dad works for you! Completely true statement!"

"Doesn't matter. The men that work for me are *men*. A man doesn't say *anything* to a fellow man he isn't willing to back up with a right cross and definitely doesn't humiliate him in front of other people unless he wants an enemy for life. Sure, they might 'work' for you someday, but if you want them to respect you enough to actually follow orders you had best start acting like a *man*. If you don't figure that out by the time that shiner heals you'll get another soon enough and deserve it for being the *real* dumbass."

Offender of Norms suitably chastened, order and justice would be restored. The principals and coaches knew what the score was. To the Enforcer of Norms they would issue the kind of token punishment which, provided it was borne with appropriate stoicism, ensured his stature would be enhanced by the incident and still merit attaboys twenty years hence.

A combination of lung cancer and cirrhosis felled Andrew McKay in

1989. A Peace Dinner anniversary without him was unimaginable. Coincidently an election year in Rust, Assembly of Councilors Speaker Norman "Trey" Selbsteiger, III noted that Rust had never established a proper Labor Day holiday and proposed July 30th henceforth be "McKay Day." A close political ally counter-proposed that such a day ought rightly recognize Selby as well, and over Trey's distinctly half-hearted objections July 30th became McKay-Selbsteiger Day, to this day a national holiday in Rust.

To return to the original Peace Dinner of 1975, Selby had reasons beyond the pecuniary to bury old animosities. Trey's talents were much more social than managerial, and the family had long recognized that the health of the Widget Company, or of any family business interests for that matter, was far too important to ever entrust to his stewardship. Politics however was an arena in which he could excel. Selby needed to ensure Trey's triumphant return from college would see him elected to Rust's Assembly of Councilmen.

Trey had been sent to Cambridge for his edification, where he received a straight set of Gentleman's Cs, being more interested in the set of Ladies' Cs. Cambridge served Trey as the winter quarters from which he would sally forth every spring to embark on a great *chevauchée* across New England. Trey may have singlehandedly destroyed single-sex higher education by systematically pillaging every single women's college east of the Appalachians, gaining admittance into each after reducing their meager defenses in a matter of days. He was in the third year of such campaigning and had amassed more booty though mounted marauding than the Black Prince could have ever imagined possible. This caused no shortage of family consternation. At one Thanksgiving Trey floated the idea of going to Hollywood after graduation only to be icily reproached by his mother that the only movie for which he was suitable would be a B-rate sequel entitled *Seven Sons for Seven Sisters*.

Besides the issues begotten by Trey, Selby's daughter Cornelia had aspirations too exalted for Rust. For her Selby had in mind Rust's UN Ambassadorship, which would let her live in New York at state expense, indulge her passion for charity with *other* people's money, and perhaps meet a nice Parisian boy on a diplomatic passport whose family vineyard was not too far from Marseilles. For both Trey and Cornelia Selby needed universal goodwill in Rust.

The final reason for valuing labor peace was that it was time to take the company public. The capital required for the expansion had stretched the Selbsteigers thin, and Katz wished to cash out. His fortune, especially valued at a public company's earnings multiple, was an order of magnitude larger than any amount he could ever live with himself for spending. It was time to end his long sojourn and return unto the land of his fathers and kindred.

The universe of said kindred was not quite as numerous as the stars he was out of the business of reaching but was expanding at a comparable rate. The House of Katz had (including himself and his wife) numbered seven upon his arrival in Rust but had since expanded by four grandchildren with three more on the way. It now offered a wide range of professional services in the New York-Newark-Jersey City MSA including investment banking, corporate litigation, forensic accounting, and dentistry. There were *a lot* of Katzes to be herded, and their matriarchs insisted this could only be done properly from Queens.

(Katz's *other* son Hampton had returned to "Nineveh." That by itself was tolerable; little Hampton had gotten bit by the politics bug as a congressional page and remained deeply earnest about the public interest. What was intolerable was taking a job writing speeches for a *Republican* senator. Katz hated the commies like any other red-blooded American—hell, he had devoted fifteen years of his life to keeping those godless gulagers on the other side of the Fulda Gap—but *that* was just too far. Why couldn't he work for Pat instead?)

Selby's grand celebration for the Widget Company of Rust's (RUST-EX: WCR) IPO was supposed to be the event of the year. It coincided with Spring Break, and Trey surprised the family by actually coming home for it instead of despoiling some Caribbean resort town. He *really* surprised the family by introducing them to him his (*WHAAAAAAAT???*) fiancée.

The soon-to-be Mrs. Anne Selbsteiger—excuse me, Ms. Anne *Altmire* Selbsteiger—had met Trey during their senior year of undergraduate studies. Trey's valedictory campaign of studying undergraduates had reached as far afield as the Philadelphia-Camden-Wilmington MSA, his previous razzias having laid waste to all the fertile fields more proximate to Cambridge. Anne was the ambitious type who no longer possessed any undergarments spared the Bonfire of Patriarchal Oppression. Nevertheless she found herself enthralled by a boy who *truly* appreciated liberated women.

She learned thralldom/liberation was a dialectic two missed periods later. Anne was of course *very* aware of the *choice* recently afforded her by the emanations and penumbras of the legal profession. She was of a mind to exercise it given her intent to devote three more academic years towards entering that profession. But... a black prince was still a prince, and a womyn doesn't get the chance to marry one of those very often. The chi—*fetus*—in her womb made her a princess. Synthesis resolved, law school could wait.

Trey was caught cold when Anne proposed the idea to him but warmed to it upon reflection. He knew the old saw about hypocrisy being the tribute vice pays to virtue and had come to realize that to succeed in politics even he would have to start paying that tribute sooner or later. The time for "later" was running short. He needed the respectability being a husband and father would confer. And Anne… she was undeniably an exceptionally intelligent and capable woman. Together they would be a formidable team.

The Altmires took the news better than the couple expected. They had despaired of ever having grandchildren, and the pregnancy relieved not only that fear but the related one as to whether Anne was even into men at all. Trey was not exactly the kind of man they would have selected for her had it still been the 14th century, but he was gregarious and polite when he needed to be. His family's wealth spared them the obligation to finance a law degree which would have been an in-kind donation to every political cause they disdained. Their contribution to the wedding was to procure the services of New York's most talented photographer, who ensured posterity saw gleaming white rather than real-life eggshell and artfully disguised any awkward visual evidence the rules of propriety had been bent.

Selby, flush from his recent liquidity event, lavished more on the wedding than his business sense thought appropriate for what he was trying to tell himself was an "investment." The invitations were so thick the postal service charged him freight rates (*thank goodness* those had been negotiated well). The stationery for the thank-you notes was less supple but more legal tender. A nice thank-you note goes a long way with people, and Trey's fall swearing-in was as well-attended as his spring nuptials.

Anne stayed out of Rustan politics for the first few years. Balancing her by-correspondence legal studies and the motherhood of her daughter Drew (Anne's whole-life commitment to the project of permitting no space from which men could exclude women included the namespace) was already two full-time jobs. Anne could have, had she wished, pursued those studies in person. The Selbsteigers had the resources, and Grandma Louisa was positively *eager* to look after Drew. That however was precisely what Anne did not wish.

Anne and Louisa's relationship developed into one akin to that between superhero and supervillain (who was whom depended on perspective), in which they had the mutual admiration and respect afforded the sole enemy sufficiently dangerous to constitute a legitimate threat. Unlike the pulpy characters who dealt with trifles like biological superweapons and corporate empires, their duel had truly cosmic stakes: the rearing and formation of Drew. Anne took the aphorism about possession being nine tenths of the law as a core principle.

Considered as an investment, the performance of Trey's political career was superb. It reached positive cashflow from operations almost immediately, could cover capital expenditures within three years, and matured enough to initiate a dividend by year five, an impressive feat given the T&E budget. When Anne was ready to join the firm as equity partner, the acquisition was highly accretive. She had no shortage of clients in Rust, for whom she had an exceptional record of securing advantageous settlements. It would only take a few years of compound growth to become the pre-eminent power couple of Rust.

Silver

The 81-82 recession was a shock to the equilibrium. It got bad enough Selby reluctantly furloughed workers rather than countenance a first-ever dividend cut or floating notes at 16%. Fortunately, morning eventually rose, and he smoothed over hard feeling expressed at the Peace Dinner anniversary with back wages. While the idea of cutting the dividend was anathema, never again would he be able to raise it. Top-line sales were now growing by the inflation rate of—praise and glory be unto to that giant—only 4%.

But that situation was... fine. *So what* if his P/E was only 7? The dividend from Selby's majority stake was more than enough to cover the social and charitable obligations that accrued to Louisa's and his positions. The majority stake also meant no corporate raider could take it away from him. *So what* if the workforce had a little redundancy? Do they really not want him providing jobs? *So what* if he couldn't explain in detail what all his VPs did? Did those dumbasses not understand delegation?

The mid-80s also begat Norman Selbsteiger, IV (*phew*). It really was the mid-80s that begat Norman IV because Anne insisted on IVF. It wasn't a fertility problem (*definitely* not that), nor was it an attraction problem. Rather, it was a kind of attraction problem: Trey had his roguish charm, but despite her diligence Anne didn't quite know everywhere Trey's roguish charm had been. The 70s had been a different time. Gonorrhea, chlamydia, and even syphilis were easily treatable with antibiotics. Now there were scarier things out there. Herpes… that's forever. Hepatitis… eesh. And AIDS? A *little bit* of danger is sexy, but it's hard to climax worrying about the risk of having to tell the kids Mom is going to waste away and die on them because their father didn't like condoms.

Norman IV's birth also marked the final severing of Norman III's relationship with his mother. Upon inspecting the birth certificate, Louisa remarked—in front of the assembled family and hospital staff—that *that* name was only proper for a *first* son.

The sign of having truly made it in politics is the real estate deal. Titles and offices are fine and dandy, but the sweetheart investment opportunity is the real validation of power. It signals unmistakably the acquiescence of people with money that they need you more than you need them. The old guard in the Assembly had come out quite well from the highway treaty, but that had been over two decades ago. Over that time the economic center of gravity in Rust had shifted away from the lakefront, leaving it increasingly moribund amidst the general prosperity. The blighted shoreline had become an embarrassment for Rust.

Redevelopment solved a lot of problems for a lot of people. Rust had no shortage of VPs who could afford to buy a weekend family getaway and no shortage of developers positively *eager* to sell them one provided the lakefront be rezoned. There was a younger generation in the Assembly that hadn't yet gotten their bite at the apple. After a couple plots apiece for a quorum-worth at the worthless-while-zoned-industrial price, "A New Vision for Rust's Lakefront" could propel Trey's long-awaited ascension to the speakership.

The lakefront also solved the weekday problem of happy hour at Metzger's. No one spends two hours getting dolled up and two more pretending to like martinis and wood paneling at a meat market in order to hear, "so how about *your* place?" On buy side, during a late night at the office, blowing through bills at the bar only begets being blown off, and blowing through bills in the bathroom only begets being blown. The deal can only be consummated at "my place on the lake."

For Trey, aside from shoring up his power base, there was basic comfort. What's the point of becoming a head of government if you're still sleeping on the couch? Anne had always been the detail-oriented one, and as valuable as that was it caused its own set of problems. Those could be greatly eased with a cashflow she didn't know about to cover expenses best left off bank statements she scrutinized. The fees she was going to get from all the legal work, the best plots near the soon-to-be marina, and below-cost construction for their own place were enough that she wouldn't automatically assume Trey was hiding anything else.

The key to a good deal is the thinly-capitalized third-party contractor. Its purpose is to transfer at arms-length a completely reasonable package of risk and reward into a limited-liability entity with nowhere near enough capital to cover any liabilities. Selbsteiger & Son Shipping was still technically a going concern, albeit only in the business of delivering tax losses. Title to the entity had long since been transferred to Trey for estate-planning purposes as it would be much cleaner down the road to transfer assets to *it* rather than Trey personally.

It did however still own the abandoned docks which were to be redeveloped into the marina and boat club as the centerpiece of the lakefront. Recent changes to environmental law rendered it unwise to undertake any transaction necessitating soil testing on land used for decades to ship industrial materials, so title would have to remain in the entity. It would *sell* the structures but *rent* the *use* of the land for a percentage of the dues collected by the boat club (membership in which would naturally be mandatory for the entire development). It's also unwise for a thinly-capitalized third-party contractor to be overtly eponymous, so before anything was inked Selbsteiger & Son Shipping would be reestablished in an anonymity-friendly jurisdiction as Third Person Limited LLC.

By the turn of the decade, the stock market mostly resolved the tension between the Efficient Market Hypothesis and single-digit P/Es on the numerator side. For the Widget Company of Rust the denominator did the heavy non-lifting. The passing of Andy McKay, while not exactly a surprise, was an uncomfortable *memento mori* for Selby. It was time for him to get serious about the future of his company and his family. Louisa was reaching the life stage where she wished to begin receding from social prominence in order to dote on her grandchildren, which required travel.

It would have been deeply unwise to abdicate in favor of Trey. It wasn't merely the awkwardness of resigning a head-of-government position for a promotion; the problems with Trey ran deeper. To even give him legal title had become too risky: not only was that too openly glaring a conflict of interest for the Assembly to stomach, it was also asking to forfeit half in short order unless he cleaned up his act. There weren't a whole lot of good options.

It wasn't sexist prejudice that prevented Cornelia from taking over the company. Selby and the physically enfeebled but still lucid Norman, Sr. discussed that possibility at length, for the time of the female executive had arrived. Cornelia's post-UN tour of NGOistan had produced a resume of management experience that had grown quite impressive. There were limits to its applicability, however. Soliciting donors over tartare and sparkling chardonnay in Saint-Tropez was in some sense *like* cutting deals over chop steaks and boilermakers at Metzger's, but the thought of Cornelia Selbsteiger de Ruille going from the former to the latter just did not compute.

There were social issues as well: the burghers of Rust were not going to take the relaxed European view of Jacques's (tastefully singular) Milanese mistress. Speaking of, what on earth would *Jacques* have to do in Rust? International viticulture does not exactly ascribe *terroir* to the soil of industrial towns, and he wasn't about to start drinking beer. Then there were the logistics: running the Widget Company was an in-person, face-to-face job. Cornelia's family and social obligations were too geographically diffuse for that. One couldn't just be absent for the *whole month* of August. She could be a superb board chair, but an executive role was unworkable.

The ultimate reason Selby sold WCR was that he knew the changes it required to survive. Regardless of who was or was not suited to the job, they were changes *no* Selbsteiger could make given their place in Rust. While certainly wealthy, Selby did not consider himself a greedy man; he took a comparatively modest salary, relying instead on the dividend for his income. Taking more out of the company would have been pointless: that which he wished to purchase could not be acquired by ordinary transaction, only by generosity in employment. That system required profits with which to be generous, and those were in ever shorter supply. To restore them the Widget Company needed an infusion of fresh capital for upgrades and a leaner, more efficient workforce.

Selby sat in the conference room while the artists formerly known as corporate raiders (not PC to say that to their faces) played that stupid make-*you*-wait-on-*us* power game. He pondered the irony the he, private citizen majority owner, was about to sell his company to an investment firm managing the pension money of teachers and firemen, yet it was for *them* the transaction was termed "private equity." The only salve for the sensory deprivation torture was one of those faddish Magic Eyes that were *everywhere* now. Selby took the bait and stared into the cyclical stereogram. By the time the image resolved into a fish, the sharks deigned to enter the tank.

 "You don't seem to enjoy Boston as much as your son."

"I wasn't aware you were friends."

"I wouldn't say 'friends.' We had to PNG him from the house junior year."

 "Shall we get to business?"

"You mean now, after five years of not taking our calls? I suppose we should thank you. We're paying half what you'd have gotten then. It's cost you a lot to make him mayor."

"Speaker."

"Oh, right, how could I forget? They call his place on the Vinyard 'The Consulate' because you can't go barge in and arrest a head of government this side of the tropics. He makes even the senator jealous."

"Watch it there. Our pond may be smaller than yours, but no one's fishing bodies out of it on his account."

"Your pond? Your pond is evaporating, old man, which is why it's about to be *our* pond."

"You're buying the company, not the city. He's still the Speaker, and you'll still be dealing with him and Anne long after you're done with me."

"You really think he can make it without you?"

"*So what* if I got him his start? He's his own man, stood on his own two feet for fifteen years now."

"Around here he's not known for staying on his feet for long. I took you for a shrewder man. Enjoy your retirement, Mr. Selbsteiger. The fall is prettier here. Maybe he can show you."

Norman Selbsteiger, Jr. (Founder, Chairman) and Cornelia Selbsteiger de Ruille (President, CEO) jointly cut the ribbon. In the gallery of notables, Louisa (director) was beaming. Jacques (honorary, non-voting director) was politely bored. Drew (directorship to become active upon majority) was distraught. Little Norman, Marie, Jacques *fils*, and Sophie (directorships to become active upon majority) were cute in the way only formally dressed children trying their best to sit still can be. Even the aged Norman Selbsteiger, Sr. (honorary co-Chairman) came out for a likely final public appearance. The Selbsteiger Foundation was open for business. Selby may have sold out of the widget business, but he was not selling out of Rust.

Norman Selbsteiger, III (Vice Chairman) could not attend the ceremony, which was just fine with everyone who could. He was being deposed. Anne Altmire's (plaintiff) divorce filing had hit the docket within hours of the Selbsteiger Foundation's incorporating paperwork. She had accumulated so much evidence over so many years it took a freight carrier (much cheaper now thanks to deregulation) to get it all to the courthouse. This was not a no-fault affair.

Trey was notionally still Speaker but was the lamest of ducks; it merely remained to negotiate the terms of departure. It is one thing to "have heard unsubstantiated rumors" but another to have all it laid out in court documents. With deniability no longer plausible the fire and brimstone rained down about him. Pardon was out of the question; there had to be *some* punitive consequence. They found a novel one— rather, an archaic one—satisfactory to all parties. Shortly after the calendar turned, the Rust Assembly of Councilors accepted the resignation of Norman Selbsteiger, III. It then by unanimous vote issued a writ of outlawry.

The colloquial use of *outlaw* is imprecise. The desperados of the Wild West, e.g., were *like* outlaws as fugitives from justice, but unlike medieval English courts frontier law did not issue formal writs of outlawry even if de facto practice was similar. Outlawry proper is a legal practice which withdraws all protection of the law, which in English common law could be done as criminal punishment or for refusal to obey a summons. An outlaw could be robbed, assaulted, or even killed with impunity.

The default constitutional position is that legal instruments valid within English common law at the time of the founding are still operative unless specifically abolished. Outlawry was then a live if infrequent practice in Britain, which did not end it formally until the 1930s. Unlike bills of attainder, the Constitution does not explicitly forbid writs of outlawry, nor has any treaty terminated the practice a la letters of marque and reprisal. Issuing them is not a power granted to congress, but neither is it denied to the judiciary.

The 14th amendment forbids *states* to "deny to any person within its jurisdiction the equal protection of the laws" which categorically prevents *states* from reviving the practice. However it has never been litigated whether the *federal government* could do so in federal territory, as there has never been a test case; federal criminal statutes and sentencing guidelines have never employed writs of outlawry. Arguments would have to revolve around the 5th and 8th amendments. Founders' intent is inscrutable; neither the Federalist Papers nor Madison's notes discuss outlawry. Rust was not a *state* in the sense used by the 14th amendment, nor is the Assembly *congress*, and its legal harmonization treaty afforded it the general prerogatives of the *federal government* circumscribed by the Constitution.

So at least went the argument made to the skeptical US Ambassador. After consultation he informed Rust Washington would not then contest the interpretation but reserved the option to do so in the future should it deem warranted. The 14th amendment would however protect the outlaw within the territories of the several states.

The cuts at WCR Industries (just "WCR" now, standing for nothing) came down afterwards. Its new ownership concluded that after equipment upgrades it required only half of its previous workforce and even less of its previous management.

Selby would never have done such a thing.

Bronze

There are only so many places for disgraced, former head of government to go. The Potomac Basin was perfect; Trey, like most, preferred to live amongst his kind. He could have, had he wished, challenged the writ from his comfortable exile. He had no shortage of appellate acquaintances at the Ashmont Birchford CC positively *eager* to take such a novel case. His own opinion was that his punishment, while certainly unusual, was not especially cruel. It stung to sell The Consulate, but that was more about the loss of immunity than loss of legal personhood.

He derived a certain enjoyment from his new status. Plenty of women are attracted to bad boys, but to be the first legally declared Anglophone outlaw in a century? Dude, that is *sick*. *So what* if they got herpes? There were drugs for that now. In any event challenging the writ would be a costly, 54-month procedure for which the diminished cashflow from Third Person Limited was inadequate.

The Potomac Basin was also clearly a much better place for little Norm. Unlike his sister, Norm (as he liked to go by) actually wanted to be with his father and was too young to understand why people made that sucking-air-through-their-teeth sound when he said so. Anne was amenable to allowing Trey custody because her own overwhelming matriarchal concern was closely managing the undergraduate education, future legal education, and subsequent public-interest/political career of Drew. Even were it an option, Rust would have been a terrible place to raise Norm. There he would have been forever burdened by the sins of his father, haunted by the ghosts of his aborted half-siblings, and not even able to get a full year's worth of advanced credits. In the Potomac Basin, he could have an ordinary childhood amongst the legitimate progeny of senators and ambassadors and a doctor's note authorizing all the extra time and pharmaceutical assistance required to earn a double-700 credential.

Among the lessons Trey had learned from his ex was the value of paying extremely close attention to legal detail. Technically, a writ of outlawry merely demotes the legal status of the outlaw to that of a wolf; complete loss of protection followed from wolves' standing in medieval law. In modern law however, a wolf could enjoy substantial legal protection provided it was a member of an endangered species. Such status would not restore Trey's standing to sue or his property rights in Rust, but it would make shooting him on sight once again felonious. He didn't expect to *need* this protection, but it was nice to have in the event he ever had business to conduct there or within the District proper. The case for recognizing the Rustan Wolf as endangered was completely straightforward: 1) it was a distinct species, being unable to produce fertile offspring with any other member of the genus *Canis*, 2) it was numerically tiny, and 3) it was clearly under threat in its natural habitat.

The natural habitat of the Rustan Wolf was of course the entirety of Rust, the establishment of which was a coterminous consequence of granting it endangered status. Any significant development in Rust would now have to perform an environmental impact assessment to ensure it would not adversely affect said habitat. *That* was expensive and time-consuming. It was much cheaper—but certainly not free— to secure an attestation directly from the Rustan Wolf to that effect, possible because uniquely among endangered species the Rustan Wolf had command of the English language and of legal detail. For a sub- stantially greater fee the Rustan Wolf was willing to attest that a par- ticular parcel of real estate was not its natural habitat at all.

Anne's divorce made her a cause célèbre. It was the first time a woman had ever taken down a head of government that way, and if that wasn't exactly true it didn't matter. *So what* if Isabella of France had *technically* pulled it off a little earlier? Such pedantry had no place in the time of First Times. The speaking circuit only lasts so long though, and Anne had fourteen years to burn (five to re-establish citizenship, nine more for eligibility) before she could enter the Senate. She also needed more money. She had a lifestyle to maintain, and senate campaigns are *expensive*.

The difference between a rich boy and a rich man's son is substantial in divorce proceedings, especially when the rich man's son has no assets whatsoever in Rust because he is legally lupine. For all the fireworks in Anne's filing, the case was mooted: marriage law in the 90s did not recognize trans-species couples. The marriage was not dissolved but invalidated. Title to all property in Rust previously held jointly defaulted to Anne, but that was the end of it. One cannot get alimony from a canid, nor can one take half in jurisdictions where said canid retained his legal personhood and property rights when there hadn't technically been a divorce.

The Rustan property Anne could claim wasn't worth much anymore in a flooded market. Half the ex-neighbors were ex-VPs attempting alienation to finance their own emigrations. It didn't help that Anne's nice lakefront place was now infamously nicknamed "The Doghouse." After a couple of fruitless years, the maintenance, headache, and property taxes stopped being worth the hassle, so she just defaulted on the taxes, handed title over to the land authority, and washed her hands of the situation.

On the speaking circuit top dollar came from The Street, in no small part due to its pre-existing admiration for Anne's famously legendary stock-picking on the RUSTEX. The Street also highly prized people who paid extremely close attention to legal detail. It was a perfect match. Anne's legal acumen became invaluable to the burgeoning business of bespoke securities. Legal knowledge alone however isn't enough for that business; one must also master the minutia of accounting and finance.

Ms. Altmire was up to the challenge. The first key to a successful novel financial product is its accounting asset level. On a balance sheet, Level 1 assets are things like stocks and bonds, which have deep and liquid markets and can therefore be valued at market price. Level 3 assets are the esoteric concoctions requiring large reserves and extensive disclosure. Level 2 is the goldilocks place in between. An ordinary-life analog is a house: one can always know the value of a house within a reasonable margin of error. To actually transact a house at that value normally takes weeks and might take months. There is a useful rule of composition for more complex assets: a product composed entirely of Level 2 assets is also Level 2. If a house is Level 2, so is the entire neighborhood.

Barrier options are derivative financial products in this Level 2 classification. At their simplest, barrier options have the form "If security X ever reaches price Y within time-window T, then $Z is paid, all-or-nothing." Even in this simplest case they are extraordinarily complex to value, so they aren't traded enough to be Level 1. In more complex form, "$Z" can be replaced with any financial product, making the barrier option a conditional wrapper around nearly anything. In order to keep a basket of them from becoming Level 3, there had to be a rule: nothing exotic.

The ichor of Olympian finance is credit. When two counterparties trade a derivative product, if they wait until the product expires to settle up, then they are relying on each other's credit. The opposite of credit is margining. When a product is margined, cash is exchanged every day based on the change in market value. The closest real-life analogue to margining/credit choices is the relationship between bettor and bookie: a bettor generally prefers to bet first and settle up later, but the bookie will only allow this when he's confident the bettor is good for it.

The key difference occurs in bankruptcy. If a product is margined, any owed cash has already changed hands. The non-bankrupt counterparty can transact the same product again at current market without incurring a loss. Things get messy when one side of a non-margined trade goes bankrupt. If the bankrupt counterparty is the creditor, then they get paid in full. If the non-bankrupt counterparty is the creditor, then they get in line with all the other creditors and fight it out in court.

Anne's most clever idea involved margining rules. The Street called it (*never* in emails—they were no dummies) "the slide": a *margined* basket of barrier options on *unlikely* events sounded like a flexible, customizable, insurance-like product which paid out in advance of the insured event as it became increasingly more likely. This was what they told regulators it was for and a completely legitimate purpose. A *non-margined* basket of barrier options on *highly likely* events sounded instead like a bond: the seller received premium up front and paid out in the future as the barrier options predictably struck. However it wasn't debt to the seller. Because the liability was technically *conditional*, it belonged in the vaguer, more flexible accounting category of reserves. This was its real purpose.

The true artistry of the slide was that margining rules for over-the-counter derivatives are not set by the terms of the product itself; they are set by the umbrella trading agreements between counterparties. The exact same product could function in dramatically different ways by changing its context. Because the slide could produce a wide range of sounds, they had to give it an appropriate backronym: TRadable Outstanding Multiple Barrier Option with Nothing Exotic. The Street (and Anne) made *a lot* of money off TROMBONEs.

The TROMBONE's maiden performance was financing the buyout of WCR Industries. Its owners considered the turnaround a success, and it was now their wish to turn around and clear their hurdle on schedule. The surprise high bid came from a defense contractor. The peace dividend of the 90s had not been especially great for *their* dividend, so they had branched out into businesses where they would have synergies. It wasn't absurd to think they might achieve these in medium-tech consumer durables. What was absurd was the value they seemed to place on WCR's old development archives, apparently applicable to their next generation of GPS-integrated defense offerings.

The ensemble needed a TROMBONE because while "synergy" sounded great to investors, the debt consequent to the high bid did not. The preferred sound was "muted": enough collateral to make the don't-call-it-debt non-recourse to the holding company, who would therefore not need any reserves on its balance sheet. The equity and assets of the once-again profitable WCR were adequate for this purpose. Thus did WCR Industries become, after securing the customary attestation from the Rustan Wolf, a subsidiary of LABANCO.

LABANCO struggled to match the success of WCR's previous management, much less achieve the anticipated synergies. From a shop floor view one might suppose swapping three-button suits for two-button ones wouldn't change much, but the new suits were tailored to different incentives. Previous management's ultimate compensation had been tied to the eventual company sale price, which maintained clarity and focus. They were hard-edged and cold-eyed people who had laid off half the plant, so labor relations were never exactly *good*, but they knew labor peace was a necessary condition to achieve both the efficiencies and stability requisite to realize that value. They were also few in number and fixed in their roles, so the workers at least knew the lines of accountability.

The conglomerate style of LABANCO sought synergy cycling management through its various businesses to transfer best practices, resulting in a managerial class of sound methodological but nonexistent domain expertise. Rust was not exactly a prime posting, so the ambitious climbers proving their complete, self-abnegating loyalty to The Company by accepting it had an out-of-sight, out-of-mind problem. The solution was placing maximum effort into getting facetime at HQ to talk about what a great job they were doing and minimum effort into actually doing said job. The ideal way to demonstrate one was a "difference maker" to senior management was to affect a reorganization. Those necessitated extensive presentations with a "core future" featuring a gracefully upward exponential curve and a "legacy" featuring a table in 7-pt font in the appendix on slide 81.

Perpetually transitioning into the re-imagined future disoriented the workers, who had to operate in a tense present without clarity regarding who was in charge of what. In any event the two-buttons were usually in the Potomac Basin walking through a deck entitled, "Reconceptualizing the New Paradigm of Workflow: A Synthesis of Innovative Metrics and Practices." Labor relations also soured for other reasons. Most employee sensitivities are not matters of money but of pride, and LABANCO's managers had never learned the lessons only taught by a high school black eye. In retrospect, part of Selby's intuitive business genius had been his style of personnel—or rather, personal—management. One needn't treat them as equals, but merely by treating employees as human *beings* rather than human *resources* one could get away with quite a lot on the bottom line. Not until becoming part of LABANCO did WCR's workers encounter a modern human resources *department*. Jubilation did not ensue. Such institutions' conceptions of *sensitivity* and *pride* differed dramatically from those on the production floor.

Trey's hopes for Norm's college experience were set on Cambridge based on his own fond memories and, duh, Cambridge. There was however the matter of the reputation those fond memories had created and its interaction with where in the order of precedence Norm's application would fall. Trey was under the impression he was of rank "heads of government" where full-on biological warfare did not inhibit acceptance, so why would a couple cases of chlamydia (*easily* treatable) be a big deal? The admissions consultants delicately reminded him his rank was in fact "disgraced, former heads of government" which in the order of precedence was inferior to the other rank he held, that of "alumni board members of eponymous major charitable foundations."

Admissions informed the Selbsteigers that at rank "alumni board members of eponymous major charitable foundations" Norm's double-700 credential was "comfortably acceptable," the chlamydia was not problematic, but the precedent of admitting him was. To admit a legacy of Norman Selbsteiger, III *as such* might bind the admissions office on as much as 1.2% of an incoming class, and the order of precedence was graded too finely to accommodate that potentiality. However, were Norm to apply at the mere rank of "board members of eponymous major charitable foundations," his double-700 credential, as diminished by the chlamydia matter, would be deemed "merely acceptable, with minor charitable considerations."

Trey and Norm were taken aback. *Pere et fils* were suddenly of one mind, hit by a shockwave realization: any random hookup in the Boston-Cambridge-Newton MSA would expose Norm to an uncomfortably nontrivial risk of committing inadvertent incest. The repercussive realization was recognizing this risk as relevant to the entire Acela Corridor. Thus to Palo Alto did Norm matriculate, where at rank "board members of eponymous major charitable foundations" his double-700 credential inherited no venereal burden and was deemed "merely acceptable."

Management incentives notwithstanding, the reason LABANCO recurrently reorganized WCR was that the business was eroding. The gracefully upward exponential curve remained imaginable because global demand for widgets was indeed growing exponentially. WCR was squeezed because the global price of widgets was plummeting faster than it could cut costs. Both had a common cause: China. In the mid-90s not a single widget was produced there, but by the mid-2000s China was the largest producing country and featured no fewer than six factories capable of double WCR's all-sites output.

Investing more into the Rust site was hard to justify. The economical upgrades had already been made by previous management; to remain truly competitive would require a ground-up rebuild. The bigger problem was that the site no longer possessed strategic value. In the 70s, nearly all of the Widget Company's supply chain and a third of American consumers were within a day's trucking distance of the factory. In the world of globalized supply chains and globalized consumer markets what really mattered was proximity to an international port. The closest one to Rust was on the wrong coast for Asia and couldn't be reached in a day with the new federal 11-hour limit for truckers. To remain alive in the widget business LABANCO needed to focus on better locations with cheaper labor.

The Central Bank of Rust kept a low profile at Jackson Hole. Central bankers may or may not be overrated as economists, but they are absolutely underrated as diplomats. CBR officials didn't *really* have any business there, but they would submit research to justify their presence (usually related to commodity-currency interaction), which their counterparts accepted in spirit with the sort of polite praise one would give a well-done undergraduate senior thesis. In the mid-2000s though CBR did have business—rather, a lobbying campaign—to conduct.

LABANCO's ultimate problem in the widget business was macroeconomic. Rustan widgeteers were by raw quantity output per worker-hour ten times as productive as their Chinese competitors. At then-present exchange rates they were being paid as though they were thirteen times as productive. Widgets were sufficiently commoditized that even had LABANCO managed WCR well the situation would have still been unsustainable. Given the friction between its actual management and the union there was zero chance of achieving alignment changing nominal wages.

Process of elimination left currency as the only solution. Like many economic satellites, Rust maintained a fixed exchange rate (a "peg") between the Rustan Dollar (the "Rusty") and the US Dollar. The CBR had let the Rusty appreciate throughout the 70s, mitigating inflation and spreading the wealth created by widgets to ordinary Rustans via greater purchasing power. It had lowered the exchange rate during the

91-92 recession, the previous time WCR's condition had been alarming, but increasingly unwisely had not changed it since. The reluctance to revalue was not about loss of face but rather the size of that thirteen vs ten gap. Devaluing the Rusty that much would vaporize a quarter of middle-class Rust's wealth and induce distress in any entity indebted in USD. What Rust *really* wanted was a weaker Dollar.

They were nearly laughed out of the room. It wasn't disagreement of principle—that current account imbalances made USD depreciation inevitable was the entire premise of the conference—but of practicality. The one belief uniting the entire developing world was the intolerability of a weaker Dollar to the global economy. Forty percent of the world by Gross Domestic Product and sixty percent by population was competitively depreciating their own currencies. China was so committed to this policy it was effectively taxing its own middle class to subsidize the mortgages of America's by 150 basis points. The US had neither the desire nor the ability to pick a currency fight with half the world just to accommodate an intransigent union in Rust.

Norm needed ten minutes to calm his father down after uttering the phrase "start an incubator," but after finally clarifying he meant seeding and gestating premature *companies* pops was hella cool with it. The Rustan Wolf now had the capital for a venture like this. Norm wasn't exactly a hard worker, but he did have an eye for opportunity and paid enough attention in business classes to make a pitch. Rather than go Greek he realized that for the investment of a down payment on real estate that would probably appreciate anyway he could instead *get paid* by his fellow bros to live somewhere kicked kegs served as furniture. The real kicker was getting paid in the most precious currency in The Valley: equity.

As graduation approached, the consultancies recruited Norm like a 6-star prospect, because… that's exactly what he was. He had good (enough) grades from an elite university, a demonstrable eye for sound business strategy, a pre-existing immersion in a hot industry, and a dazzling wealth of social connections. The world had never before seen such an ideal specimen of the species *Homo Sapiens Consultus*; such perfection could not even be created in a lab. He had a couple unexpected stipulations ("No, really, I mean it. I *can't* do the Acela Corridor."), but a 6-star recruit has all the leverage so they were accepted. In The Valley Norm remained.

LABANCO's tolerance for failure at WCR ran out when the recession began. The assets weren't worth much anymore, and amidst a recession couldn't be sold for more than was owed on the TROMBONE. As said assets had been the collateral for said TROMBONE, the simplest way out was strategic default. LABANCO handed title over to The Street and washed its hands of the situation.

Heroes

The closure of the factory set in motion a macroeconomic crisis. Maintaining balance-of-payments depended critically on widgets because while they accounted for only ("only") 10% of Rust's Gross Domestic Product (which like any developed economy was majority services) they accounted for 40% of Rust's current account inflows (the services being mostly intra-Rust affairs). In the absence of inflows from widgets, maintaining the Rusty/Dollar exchange rate required CBR to buy Rustys with its reserves of Dollars. It quickly realized this was futile and would exhaust its reserves within weeks. Continued defense would only enrich macro-strategy hedge funds when they inevitably won and the CBR inevitably lost. The peg was indefensible and would have to be abandoned.

There was a break-in-case-of-emergency plan on the shelf. Managing a fixed exchange rate unchanged for sixteen years was a part-time job, so the Central Bank of Rust had war-gamed all kinds of outlandish scenarios in its free time. It had concluded that should major revaluation become necessary, stair-stepping the peg down until a stable level was found was a bad idea. That strategy would exhaust of both its USD reserves and its credibility as pegs were sequentially abandoned. Instead it was better to rip off the bandage: float the currency, wait for a market equilibrium, and only then attempt to re-establish a new fixed rate.

"Float" of course meant "sink." *How far* the Rusty needed to sink was unknown. CBR economists, based on their widget productivity estimates, figured something on the order of 25%. In the absence of widgets it was really anyone's guess. Despite having a plan, the CBR was still terrified to push the plunger because it would light the fuse on the semtex that had piled up around Ferrox.

Ferrox Financial (RUSTEX: FNFX), formerly First Bank of Rust, was Rust's biggest bank. Technically FBR still was, and FNFX was merely the holding company atop it, but that only became important later. Ferrox, being a bank, was in the business of loaning Rustys to Rustans on terms specifying when the Rustys would be repaid to Ferrox. The Ravenous Global Hunger for Yield had loaned Ferrox some very cheap capital on terms specifying when the *United States Dollars* would be repaid to the RGHfY. The long and short of it was that FNFX was long fixed-income assets yielding RST and short fixed-income assets yielding USD. A 25% adverse change to the RST/USD rate would instantly pulverize all of Ferrox's equity.

The regulators at Rustan Treasury were no dummies. They had insisted Ferrox hedge its currency risk with agreements to exchange currency at a fixed rate in the future ("currency swaps"). The other side of these swaps was The Street. They too were no dummies, could read the current account and currency reserve data just as well as the CBR could, and would only transact within a tenor of 24 months. The swaps were not going to keep Ferrox solvent, but they could keep it liquid long enough to recapitalize.

The First Bank of Rust had played a subtly important role facilitating the widget business. In the 70s widgets had been positioned as a quintessentially middle-class aspirational good, at a price point whose affordability was often contingent on financing. FBR back then had done brisk business bridging those aspirations with 12-, 24-, and 36-month offers. By the 90s widgets had become cheap enough and the Great American Middle Class wealthy and be-credit-carded enough that financing them like furniture had become faintly ludicrous. Anyone seeking to finance such a purchase was advertising themselves as an air-raid-siren credit risk.

FBR had maintained the dwindling, ossified relic of a business through the 90s out of organizational inertia, nostalgia, and because... why shut down something that still made (tiny bits of) money? An unexpected surge in widget financing began during the 2001 semi-recession. Not being at first wholly comfortable adding that kind of credit risk at scale to its own balance sheet, FBR got into securitization: pool the loans, slice the pools into tranches, and sell the tranches. Anyone with a mortgage model could change half a dozen numbers and start trading widget-backed securities. The RGHfY was introduced to WBS, and FBR's status as the only reputable institution originating such loans gave it a near-monopoly on pooling and securitizing them.

The RGHfY charged into WBS like bulls to a matador. The scale of the business outgrew the balance sheet and risk tolerance of FBR's old-school bankers, but originating and servicing widget-backed securities provided Rust with a desperately needed alternate source of current account inflows. The need for an originating company ring-fenced from the bank proper but still within the same holding company was the impetus for the reorganization and rebranding of First Bank of Rust into Ferrox Financial. The two entities had a simple corporate relationship but a complex cooperative one.

FBR insisted the comprehensive loan-level creditworthiness database underpinning the pools be the responsibility of *Ferrox*. The RGHfY had pushed the yield on these securities down to a level FBR considered insane, and FBR wanted as much full-disclosure CYA as possible in the event the default rates couldn't justify the yield. FBR's involvement was to be strictly handling the money. The second piece of CYA was that FBR wanted plausible deniability on its unwritten but very real rule that that anyone who financed a widget was such an obviously alarming credit risk they would be categorically denied any other credit.

The financing of widgets and the terrible credit risk associated therewith therefore ironically saved Rust from the worst ravages of the subprime collapse: FBR had almost no bad mortgages on its books. For this Ferrox received not a shred of goodwill but rather a cascading nightmare. The Great Recession comprehensively wrecked the widget-backed securities market. The securities performed abysmally, everyone sued everyone, and everyone lost except the lawyers.

The Rustan Treasury sued Ferrox, FBR, and The Street for discriminatory and predatory lending. No one likes a bank that says, "No." FBR had unfairly refused credit to people who needed it, except when they had extended credit to people who needed it but then found themselves trapped in debt. The database support both claims. FBR's access to it obviously demonstrated its basis for refusing credit, and its claim to not use the database for this purpose obviously demonstrated it lended irresponsibly.

The RGHfY sued The Street and Ferrox for fraud. Despite access to the database, it was someone else's fault the RGHfY had lost money on an investment. Apparently the phrase "virtually[5][6] riskless[7][8][9]" had made it into the appendix on slide 81.

The RGHfY and The Street sued Ferrox over repossession. A standard term of widget financing, in the old days FBR had included it with the understanding it was an *option*, but one exercised increasingly rarely as the costs of repossession wiped out almost any value to be had via resale. The Street's securities lawyers did not grasp this subtlety but rather made clear that any failure to repossess would breach its servicing obligations and expose Ferrox to make-whole liabilities on the pools. Ferrox argued repossession at scale was value-destroying (not to mention pointlessly cruel to the hard-pressed, predominantly low-income defaulters) but couldn't overcome the plain language of the contracts. Thus, despite no malice aforethought on Ferrox's part, a substantial number of poor folks had their garages broken into and their widgets taken by repo men for no purpose except to rot away on the outskirts of Rust in a hastily-organized warehouse Ferrox had to manage.

The RGHfY and Ferrox sued The Street over the valuation models. The rating agencies had assumed full-value resale for "refurbished" widgets but had somehow neglected to incorporate any costs associated with the logistics of "refurbishment." It was on this basis that "virtually[5][6] riskless[7][8][9]" had been included in the appendix on slide 81. In the depths of a recession, sales of brand-new, not-repossessed widgets plummeted enough that the refurbs couldn't be resold for anything close to model value when they could be resold at all. The models' inaccuracy was allegedly responsible for both the loss on resale and the value-destroying costs of refurbishment.

FBR and Ferrox sued *each other* over which entity was responsible for the warehouse. Under legal siege by the RGHfY, The Street, and the government which was soon to become their new boss, this was primarily internal corporate politics over who would take the fall. There were some tangible costs, but the big one was reputational: for a brief, easily forgettable period the warehouse was adopted by the *Occupy* movement as symbolically important. Rust's annoyingly still-resident non-citizen population hadn't had a The Man to whom It could be Stuck for going on two decades and was thrilled to relive their glory days. Possession being 90% of the law, Ferrox's hasty organization of the warehouse in its own name became a liability.

Amidst the 54-month legal *bellum omnium contra omnes* came Ferrox's deepest humiliation. Ferrox achieved tactical victory in one skirmish arguing the value-maximizing choice for the refurbs in the warehouse was to liquidate them for scrap. Only then did it discover the copper wiring stripped and stolen, rendering the scrap value somewhere between nugatory and negative and rendering Ferrox legally negligent for the loss, having been dumb enough to hold the warehouse in its own name. The liability was modest, but as Ferrox had by then been effectively nationalized, covering it came at public expense. The Rustan public was not pleased to be informed it was on the hook for further expenses incurred by its bankers' ineptitude at something so basic to finance as stuffing extraneous liabilities into thinly-capitalized third-party contractors.

(One security guard's cousin, forced out of the meth business by the tracking of pseudoephedrine purchases and a two-year stint in the clink, was known to cruise around town in a black lowrider with custom copper-plated rims & bumpers ("because Coppertop's always got the juice, man") and a "LUV COPS" vanity plate. He claimed to be into payday lending nowadays but lacked a fixed place of business or any incorporated entity. Rust's law enforcement community was pretty sure it was not *they* who were this fellow's immortal beloved (literal immortality being a property of group XI transition metals) but could never satisfactorily prove what everyone suspected.)

When the CBR announced the abandonment of the currency peg the Rusty immediately fell 30% versus the Dollar. The controlled demolition was underway, and FBR's equity capital was, as expected, a puff of fine particulate. Corporate structure then became relevant: FBR was the entity its regulators cared about because that's where Rustan's bank accounts were. The regulators had wanted its books clean of any complicated derivatives, so the umbrella trading agreements between

Ferrox and The Street, to which the currency swaps were subject, were therefore between *Ferrox* and The Street. The RGHfY had offered *FBR* the cheap capital, as it was the actual bank with all the nice banky things like access to a central bank window, a portfolio of fixed income assets, and an implicit guarantee due to being (by Rustan standards) too big to fail. So, it was the *First Bank of Rust's* capital wafting away and *Ferrox Financial* standing to gain from the currency swaps.

The next stage of the plan was a cleverly disguised bailout: The Rustan Treasury announced a guarantee of certain liabilities of FBR. Highlighted was the guarantee of Rustans' bank deposits. Despite being redundant due to deposit insurance, it was intended to (and did) forestall a bank run. Buried in the footnotes was the guarantee of FBR's USD liabilities.

A bank (or any company) cannot be recapitalized so long as it has what is euphemized a "capital hole." Equity takes first loss, and no one volunteers to take a guaranteed total first loss. Bank resolution (and reorganization bankruptcy) exists to solve this very problem. However, resolution for FBR would have paralyzed too many bank accounts and required substantial government money anyway pursuant to deposit insurance. By guaranteeing the USD debt Treasury could fill in the hole, allowing FBR to raise new capital, stay in business, and eventually earn back the don't-call-it-a-bailout money that would hopefully never actually have to be disbursed.

The next explosion came too early and knocked out a structure the CBR and Treasury had not realized was load-bearing. In the early afternoon the rating agencies downgraded Ferrox from the first page of the phone book all the way back to the scrap yards. This action wasn't unexpected, but its speed was. Rating agencies typically ratified new information only after a multi-week process verifying that doing so was politically acceptable to their customers. That this had seemingly already been done was disconcerting, but it wasn't supposed to be a problem. The currency swaps hedging FNFX against the ongoing collapse of the Rusty meant Ferrox should have been a net creditor in its trading agreements, making its rating irrelevant.

That assumption was catastrophically wrong.

Ferrox had been greedy and devious.

Ferrox had levered up by selling TROMBONEs.

The sound of these muted TROMBONEs was that of a secured revolving line of credit. Ferrox's only meaningful (pre-TROMBONE) assets as a holding company had been the equity of FBR and its origination sub (the rest was just office furniture, a database, and a warehouse). These Ferrox had used for collateral, and its trading agreements specified that so long as FBR's equity retained a minimum value or

Ferrox maintained certain credit ratings then it could transact a large amount of derivatives on credit without posting margin.

The day's events had broken both conditions. The slide slid. The TROMBONEs were now cash-margined products. Ferrox owed the entire discounted future value of the outstanding barrier options, in cash USD, by close of business. The CBR and Treasury had thought they had two years to fix Ferrox. They now had two hours.

It was impossible to raise enough money or sell enough assets in time to meet the margin call. Ferrox as a holding company rather than a bank could not make use of the Central Bank of Rust's lender-of-last resort function. Even were it able, all potential collateral was either already spoken for or aggravating asthmatics downwind. To revoke the previously given guarantees would be a sovereign default, so that was off the table. The remaining choices were both bad.

Option 1 was to let Ferrox go bust. This would cap Treasury's losses at the recently guaranteed debt but would mean actually paying out without the currency swaps on which it was relying for USD. Another consequence would be complete loss of any control over FBR to The Street. Because of the guarantees it had minimal value again, and as its ownership was the collateral for the TROMBONEs it would be seized in a default and tied up in international bankruptcy litigation. Should it suffer any further losses then either the bankruptcy court or

The Street would put it into resolution, the exact result the bailout was intended to avoid.

Option 2 was to swallow it whole: put Ferrox into conservatorship and guarantee all its liabilities. This would restore its credit to that of the Rustan government and thereby undo the margin call. It would also keep the currency swaps active. The risk of this option was exposing Treasury to potentially much greater losses (and embroil it in a lawsuit against itself). Two hours was not exactly sufficient for due diligence on Ferrox's portfolio, so taking this option would give them the time to recapitalize but was betting on the unknown.

The pressure of time already inclined towards option 2. What sealed the deal was pressure from the US Ambassador. With the global financial system in a state of pandemic crisis, officials everywhere were taking a we're-all-in-this-together approach. Rust was expected to be a team player, and the losses rippling outward from the LABANCO default were causing enough problems already. They were all going to have to take one for the team eventually, and this was Rust's turn.

Iron

Anne Altmire's senate campaign launched to great pomp and fanfare as the last grains of silicon dioxide slid through the neck of the fourteen-year hourglass. The grand investiture processional unfortunately began amidst a *re*cession, and Anne's successful second career on The Street (where, to the delight of the tabloids, she had acquired the nickname "the She-Wolf") suddenly flipped from asset to liability. The other impediment was generational. The sands of time erode much over a decade and a half, and why exactly a divorce filing merited apotheosis had become less obvious by the late 2000s than it had been in the early 1990s.

The campaign faced a decision point. A management consultant from The Valley was of the mind that social networks would sink traditional campaigns and that they *absolutely had to* have a node on this network. Altmire informed him—in front of the assembled campaign staff— that they were experienced professionals who knew what they were doing thank you very much and *did not* appreciate the tone in which his presumptuously unsolicited advice had been arrogantly asserted.

Ms. Anne's misandry marked the final severing of the campaign's relationship with the consultant, who found her primary challenger's campaign positively *eager* for input from techbros. Despite being an Acela Corridor concern, its innovative social strategy became the talk of The Valley, which despite being full of antisocial dudes could never figure out why this particular one left so much on the table by remaining anonymous.

The campaign's makeover was a pivot back to Ms. Anne's glorious heroism in Rust, but the messaging gurus found "The Heroine of Rust," didn't produce the euphoric response they expected and couldn't get her polls back to their first highs. The campaign's problems were sizably augmented by LABANCO's default: the TROMBONE gelled Rust's travails and Anne's career on The Street into a firmly cohesive story. Rust going viral for reasons unrelated to Anne's campaign injected a toxic element which paralyzed its ability to influence media narrative. The campaign couldn't tuck away the posts wondering how it was Anne had been such a shrewd real estate investor and stock picker in Rust nor give them the right contextual shape with the arthroscopic precision they were used to with traditional media. When the primary votes were tallied, the result was tough to face: all of Anne's experience, career success, whole-life commitments, and pioneering First Timer spirit counted for nothing; her own party had dumped her for someone younger and prettier.

It was months before The Street got around to sending someone to Rust to see if any value from the remnants of WCR was salvageable. Intervening events had focused attention elsewhere. It discovered the answer was "not anymore." Rust had collectively repaid the lack of severance by severing everything movable from the site. The only things left were the empty shell and the foundation, which itself was only partially usable because someone had smashed one of the slabs. Pieces of the broken concrete became a common *memento mori* in Rust almost immediately after becoming available on online marketplaces. Inquiries to local law enforcement made clear this was not something they intended to pursue, and certainly not *their* behalf.

When the CBR and Treasury inspected the non-literal rubble strewn about Ferrox they had effectively bought sight-unseen, they realized they had merely forestalled a crisis which was going to get much, much worse. The assets FNFX purchased with the premium from the TROMBONEs turned out to be none other than widget-backed securities. To keep the securitization machine running smoothly Ferrox had found it necessary to buy assorted tranches its origination subsidiary couldn't sell. The culture clash within Ferrox/FBR had resulted in dramatically different portfolios between the two entities. Ferrox believed in the power of independent distributions to mitigate risk. FBR believed in selection bias. The kind of person who financed a widget would be first over the cliff in a recession. The tranches Ferrox had been unable to sell were unsaleable for a reason.

The securities performed poorly in a double-digit U-6 environment. They also worsened the currency problem. It was one thing for Ferrox Financial to have USD-yielding WBS balanced against USD TROMBONE liabilities to The Street. It was another for the Rustan Treasury to have those liabilities when the WBS yielded only paltry quantities of USD. It was another still when the Rusty fell to 35%, 40%, 45%, and then 50% below its pre-crisis value; the diminished tax base constituting Treasury's largest asset was RST-yielding. In theory Treasury had the ability to roll its liabilities, but the Efficient Market Hypothesis had beaten it to the punch: Rust's sovereign bonds ("oxides" in buttoned-up financial press, "oxys" on harder-edged trade floors) were trading at 16%. The math on that led over the event horizon which policymakers were now realizing Rust was hurtling towards anyway.

During the bailout negotiations with Washington, Rust's leadership encountered an unexpected socio-political problem regarding the social cachet—or lack thereof—of widgets. When the WCR factory opened, the cost of widgets placed them in the home amenity basket demarcating the boundary between working and middle class, affordable to two-thirds of American households but only 10% worldwide, nearly all first world. To have a widget in one's garage was to have "made it" into the Great American Middle Class. They were completely unknown in the third world and available only in tiny numbers with decades-long waitlists to the *nomenklatura* of the Soviet Bloc. Consequently, WCR's workers and Rust at large took immense pride from widget manufacturing. Not only had the wages of the factory lifted its own workingmen into the middle class, widgets being a quintessential middle class signifier meant their physical manufacture was in some sense literally creating the Great American Middle Class.

Rust's leaders showed up to bailout negotiations under the assumption widget manufacturing was, as it had been in the 70s, a dignified enterprise with an important connection to the Great American Middle Class, which their counterparts would *want* to save. They also figured their counterparts would shrewdly realize that the better the value of the Rusty, the less the bailout would cost them. Treasury's balance sheet was only part of the problem. To be able to support the Rusty at a value which didn't eviscerate the Rustan middle class they needed to re-open the factory somehow.

Said counterparts had a snobbier but more up-to-date view of the world. A decade into the next millennium, widgets had become so ubiquitous and inexpensive that 80% of households on public assistance had one, sending widgets' status association the way of pagers. The value-add of widget manufacturing just wasn't big enough to support middle-class incomes in meaningful numbers. Widget manufacturing was so commodified and low-tech that the labor didn't even need to be literate, making it more suitable for raising Southeast Asian peasantry from rice-paddy subsistence farming poverty to the less-malnourished level of child-labor sweatshop poverty. While no one ever said it out loud, the shock of realizing how far the status of widgets had fallen in the world was what truly crushed Rust's collective sense of self-worth.

Washington's socio-political problem was, regardless of any policy stance towards the bailout (best captured by "reluctantly necessary"), it had to justify giving taxpayer money to people who were a) most famous for a cheap, disposable product, b) recently infamous for siccing repo-men to reclaim cheap, disposable products they hadn't even made, c) technically not even Americans, and d)—related to c)—still home to a small but obnoxiously loud aging "commune" of hippie draft-dodgers who had been too proud, smug, and settled-in to accept Carter's pardon (the commune had long since re-domesticated into monogamy and single-family housing but maintained its *espirit de corps*).

Despite its disdain for the déclassé, Washington did make a real attempt to come up with a plan to re-open the factory. Multiple teams of consultants (a disproportionate number of whom happened to return many rows in an FEC database query) were retained for this purpose, but all came to the same conclusion The Street had several months previously: there was simply nothing left to salvage. Any manufacturing business there was effectively starting from scratch. The factory site itself was worth less than nothing; no new business would want its associated potential liabilities. They also all came to the same conclusion LABANCO had: there was no strategic reason to locate a manufacturing business in Rust in the 21st century. Its only advantage was its cheap currency, and if un-cheapening the currency was the point of a factory that advantage would be ephemeral.

That latter conclusion was not exactly economically accurate but was necessary because such a politically sensitive report could not put in writing the real reason manufacturing could not come back to Rust. Manufacturing involves expensive equipment where even small mistakes can be both expensive and physically dangerous. In order to operate it safely one has to be sober, and it was no longer possible in Rust to recruit a workforce at meaningful scale that could pass a drug test. It had only been a year since the factory had shut down, but Rust's deterioration was progressing monthly towards the state of nature, escape from the solitude, poverty, nastiness, and brutishness of which Rustans sought chemically.

The nature of the bailout talks changed when the Rustan Treasury threatened default. The Street couldn't really afford another big credit event, and if Washington wanted to prevent that it would have to keep the USD coming one way or another. It didn't make Rust any friends, but it did get results: Washington coughed up enough to keep the government from collapsing. The downside of threatening default meant becoming a foreign aid case, and *that* meant becoming briefly occupied by NGOistan. Entirely different sets of consultants came through on their tours of duty, but the only benefit to Rust was the de facto aid provided by their spending habits.

Amidst the despair tourism was a different kind of visitor. As with archaic Greece, the epics of Rust were composed in its age of iron. Great bards came, whose muse bade them sing of the fall of Rust and of its king Manufactures, treacherously slain by (varied by bard) globalized capitalism or the collapse of middle class social values. Some brought a reporter's notebook. Some brought charts, tables, and statistical regressions. Some brought a camera. Some brought only their imagination. The story was just too perfect: the city's name, the visible profusion of literal rust, and the equally obvious decay of its infrastructure both physical and social, made it nearly trite.

The metaphor was not quite right. As a chemical process rust is not decay but a slow fire, one which will always consume its fuel so long as there is oxygen and water vapor in the atmosphere. No amount of galvanization can forever proof iron against it. It can only be held at bay by eternal, diligent, routine maintenance. It is only partially amenable to heroic acts of remediation, for oxidation is not reversible: rust can be excised but not undone. Iron, sufficiently rusted, cannot be restored; in that state it has returned to the ore from whence it came. It must be smelted down, its dross removed, and cast anew.

Epilogue

The recovery of Rust began with a text message: *Come home. We want you back.* Joshua Eckstein, Jr. had been one of the few children of Rust's professional class to return from Evanston. He shortly thereafter found himself in the Assembly of Councilors and ascended to its Speakership by the age of thirty, not by any special ambition but rather by default. He was the only person around plausibly capable of the job and willing to take it, for the Speakership had become a descent to anyone ambitious. Josh went completely gray within a few years. The job was *hard.* Governing in Rust was no longer about having a budget constraint which forced a choice between a pool and a park but rather one which forced a choice between epinephrine and naloxone.

Norm and Josh had naturally known each other as kids. Rust was small, and professional Rust was really small. Norm was never especially close with Josh, but the advent of social media had made them "friends" despite no direct contact in a decade. It also kept them apprised of each other's lives, again without any direct contact (dudebros? Cmon). But one morning, after three whiskeys alone at Metzger's, Josh reached out to the person he deemed most suited for rebuilding Rust.

It had never occurred to Norm that going "back" "home" to Rust was even an option. He'd only sort-of grown up there and hadn't even visited since he was fifteen. He had passively assumed that assuming the passive income of Third Person Limited from his late father's estate meant inheriting his PNG status as well. He was however looking for an exit strategy from The Valley; key features of the UX were being deprecated by a dev team overly indulgent of people whose philosophy of breaking things and moving fast was uncomfortably literal. Norm had seen enough of hepatitis to know he did not wish to contract it from the needles he had to step over on his walk to work. Rust's addicts at least had the courtesy to overdose indoors. He had no idea what there was for him to *do* in Rust, though.

Then it hit him.

I'll do it. I'll go home to Rust.

The old factory site was the perfect place. Norm knew it well. For reasons of obvious political sensitivity the partners at his firm had formally kept him off the Rust bailout engagement but were happy for him to be an uncredited extra in the production. One of the thinly-capitalized third-party contractors created during the WCR Industries conglomeration into LABANCO had ended up with the title to the site after

LABANCO and The Street had treated it like it was radioactive. It had long since defaulted on its property taxes and been taken into conservatorship by Rust's land management authority.

The land authority never dissolved the entity to take title because they were no dummies. The now completely un-capitalized third-party contractor served their interests just as well as it had the conglomerate's and The Street's. It would now serve Norm's equally well. The land authority, acting as conservator for the entity, would *rent* the *use* of the land to Norm at a rate which covered its property tax liability but no others and *sell* the structure to Norm for a pittance to return it to its proper, anorexic level of capitalization. As a kicker, the land authority was thrilled to finally offload to Third Person Limited the blighted lakefront properties it didn't have the money to maintain.

The thing about a post-industrial wasteland is that, provided one lays enough pavement to moot the soil's cadmium ppm level, it can be upgraded from decrepit to "gritty" on a reasonable budget. The extinction of the Rustan Wolf made redevelopment in Rust even more reasonable. Norm's contractor even found a crew willing to replace the broken slab gratis, "for old Selby's sake." *Gritty* was attractive to two types Norm wished to attract: 1) people who come from money and aren't artists but like to pretend the reverse and 2) software developers. The former were important because their autodrafts would clear and because the trendy brewpubs and bistros Rust's entrepreneurs had opened with Norm's seed capital needed a clientele ("gritty" isn't a whole-life commitment). The latter were important because an incubator isn't an incubator without nerds pumping out intellectual property.

It takes a microscope to see the intersection of the areas of interest circumscribed by those groups of people. That was OK because it was exactly where Norm wanted to be. Its existence would attract a third circle, also intersecting this sliver, the one Norm *really* needed for his project. Norm had labeled that circle with three words: *intellectual property lawyers*.

The business of seeking legal redress for infringement of patent rights was one in which Norm had by necessity as a management consultant in The Valley become a genuine expert. Like any good consultant, what truly offended him about that business was its *inefficiency*: a small company didn't have enough money to be worth the cost of going after, a medium-sized company was perfect because they could afford a settlement but not the legal fight, but the big companies were dangerous prey. An animal big enough to have FAANGs could ensure it was *you* who couldn't afford a 54-month discovery process. This was a market ripe for disruption.

Norm's moat was none other than the city-state of Rust itself. Rust's regulatory harmonization treaty with the United States meant that

Rustan patent law couldn't be changed unless the United States Senate undertook major patent reform, a prospect so ludicrous it barely merited contemplation. The treaty also required Rust to adhere to the same legal interpretations and precedents. The flip side of this treaty was that Rustan civil judgements were enforceable in the United States. The one thing Rust could—and, due to the Assembly's eternal gratitude to Norm, would—change within this system was legal *procedure*.

The central inefficiency of the system was the cost and length of time it took to go through it. A quicker legal process, which could get from filing to judgement in six months and from appeal to upholding opinion in six more would be a game changer. Any portfolio of intellectual property held by a Rustan entity with Rustan principals with clear standing to file in Rustan courts would become immensely more valuable. The system would be bulletproof because it was enabled and protected by an international treaty duly ratified by the United States Senate. Animals with FAANGs could intimidate two or three senators but not two-thirds.

The patent business was great for Norm but only meh for Rust. It brought in good money but couldn't do much for Rust's deep problems. Rust's schools were not exactly churning out patent lawyers and software developers in great numbers (the artists, talented though a handful were, were not the creditworthy kind). Norm felt he hadn't quite yet fulfilled his promises to Josh, but no matter: Rust was *his* city now, and he wanted it to succeed. What Rust needed was a Big Employer. A Big Employer meant A Lot of Capital. Norm was not there yet. A Lot of Capital meant The Foundation. The Foundation meant The Family.

Marie had followed her mother's footsteps through NGOistan, which was always thrilled to indulge people of rank "Presidents of eponymous major charitable foundations." She had married some posh triple-hyphenate whom Norm had never actually met in person. The family's dispersion necessitated that quarterly board meetings be conducted by video chat. It had been kind of a jerk move to hold the wedding on a tiny island in the Indian Ocean requiring forty hours and three layovers each way to reach *just* to make a point about its vulnerability to climate change when *some* members of the family actually had professional obligations.

In due course Marie had come back to the Foundation, and as Cornelia entered her silver years she had felt it right to abdicate in favor of her daughter. She made a fine foundation president as the role had evolved into one requiring almost purely social and personal management skills. Even if she'd possessed the financial acumen, it would have been impossible for any single human being to raise, disburse, and invest the money well. The endowment's portfolio was sufficiently complex that its management demanded a real professional, so the family had brought in a trusted one.

The clear choice for a Big Employer had to be medical. It was a growing market, Rust's existing medical infrastructure was only marginally less run-down than the rest of the city, and medicine was (in)famously labor intensive. Strictly local-focused medicine wouldn't cut it though: fixing Rust's current account problem required a destination treatment center. Rust's devalued currency would initially confer a competitive advantage: even if the medical center was as bloated and inefficient as its American counterparts it would still be a third cheaper. The Foundation already loved medical grants, so that all fit neatly together and the rest of the family could be engaged.

Cornelia would agree to any consensus, as the *emerita* would never step on her daughter's toes. Regardless, she thought the idea capital. Jacques *fils* would likewise agree to whatever. He possessed the sort of indifference only a true European could make so stylish. His only detectable passion in life was wine, so the natural thing for him to do had been to manage the vineyard. He theoretically had a wife, but she was always off somewhere exotic, doing a photoshoot and/or providing highly lucrative social media attention to an up-and-coming 5-star resort. Jacques himself clearly preferred the company of his (tastefully singular) Milanese mistress.

Drew had the unenviable problem of managing the intersection of the family Foundation of which she was a director, her (non-director) mother's strong opinions as to what she should do in that capacity, her own still frequently suffocated desire for autonomy even though she was now into middle age, and the recurring problem of men running away screaming upon encountering the preceding. She had a successful legal career, but had burned out of BigLaw and created a role at the Foundation where she took pro-bono cases. Some of these were of the earnest-desire-for-justice variety, and some were of the build-a-public-profile-that-can-be-parlayed-into-a-senate-seat variety. She was certainly not going to instigate further drama by dissention but as GC would pay extremely close attention to the legal details.

Marie and Norm had expected Sophie and Ramesh to be the hardest sells, but they turned out to be not merely invaluable to crafting the plan but positively *eager* to implement it. Sophie's interpretation of following the Foundation's commitment to medical grants had been to actually go into medical research. Even coming in at the rank of "board members of eponymous major charitable foundations" the education was servitude on a seven-year indenture. Ramesh had been a fellow such servant and the two became an inseparable pair who went into pharmaceuticals upon their indentures' fulfillment.

They made a strong point Norm hated himself for not having thought first: the recent changes to Rust's intellectual property procedure would inevitably attract an outpost of medical research. They wanted to move first and be at its center. The opportunity to build an entire industry hub around themselves was once-in-a-lifetime. Their opinion of Rust was that the inside of a lab looks the same everywhere.

Working out all the details took time. That was OK because Marie felt strongly the importance of the decision to the Foundation and its momentous implications for Rust meant the final approval needed to be in Rust and in person. Imposing a save-the-date requirement on this crowd was a harder sell than the proposal itself. The date of course *had* to be McKay-Selbsteiger Day. In any event the family had not all been together since Grandpa Selby's funeral six years ago (Uncle Trey's had not received full attendance). The vote itself would just be a formality, but formality had its place, and this was it.

On the appointed date the scattered Selbsteigers convened in Rust to hear the full and final version of The Plan. The simple version was this:

The Selbsteiger Foundation (tax-exempt non-profit) would provide at its own expense—and therefore retain title to—the real estate and the buildings for the Selbsteiger Medical Center. It would also purchase substantial amounts of surrounding real estate to accommodate future growth.

The McKay Center for Oncology (tax-exempt non-profit) would rent its share of the floorspace from the Foundation for a percentage of fees collected for providing care. The core of the MCO would be an elite team of de Ruille Fellows who would retain their affiliation with their home research hospital for their three-year Fellowship, after which they could either return or be able to write their ticket anywhere in the United States. The Fellows in more archaic language would have been called Fellow*ess*es, as the Foundation's longstanding commitment to fostering women in the highest reaches of professional life meant Fellowships would only be offered to distaff applicants. The recruiting pitch for a de Rouille Fellowship was 1) as implied, at the end any Fellow would be highly prized and competed over by major research hospitals, 2) their commitment to being in Rust (*ew*) was limited to a few years, and 3) Rust's exchange rate, *gratis* newly renovated lakefront accommodations, and the Foundation's supplementary stipend would allow them to live like duchesses for the duration of their stay. It was hoped that by law of large numbers one of the de Rouille Fellows would fall in love with either Rust, Norm, or—let's be real here— Norm's money and thereby produce both a permanent director for the MCO and a Norman, V.

The Norman "Trey" Selbsteiger, III Center for Immunodeficiency Research (tax-exempt non-profit) would, as its name suggests, engage in medical research with a focus on autoimmune diseases and seek grants through which this research would be funded. In lieu of rent for the floorspace, it would give the Foundation a 20% interest (net of any interest retained by grant-issuing governments) in any medical patents produced by the research. Any patents produced by a grant directly from the Foundation would be owned 40% by SCIMR and 60% by the Foundation. It was hoped the patent portfolio would eventually form an endowment sufficient to fund SCIMR independently.

The Aftenbridge Nursing College (tax-exempt non-profit) would educate the workforce required by the aforementioned entities and pay a fixed rent to the Foundation for its use of the facilities. Citizens of Rust would receive admissions preference. It was hoped the nursing jobs would provide a stable, secure income and just as importantly the flexible work hours needed by the single mothers who, given Rust's demographics, were expected to be the majority of students.

Ferrox Financial (for-profit C-corp, Rustan Treasury acting as conservator) would finance education at the College by offering student loans, which would then be pooled and securitized. The Foundation's endowment would receive right of first refusal on any securities underwritten by Ferrox. The Rustan Treasury would in no way guarantee the loans in the pool, but no one would mind if its conservatorship *suggested* to the RGHfY that it might. It was hoped the originating and servicing business would generate enough fees to finally pay back the Treasury's bailout money and end the conservatorship nightmare.

Details explained, President Marie put the proposal to a vote. The roll call went around the table:

Lady Marie Selbsteiger de Rouille-Aftenbridge, viscountess Ferrburn, Director, President, CEO: Aye

Mrs. Cornelia Selbsteiger de Rouille, Director, President *emerita*, honorary co-chair: Aye

Mr. Joseph Katz, MBA, CFA, Chief Investment Officer: Aye

Ms. Drew Altmire Selbsteiger, Esq., Director, General Counsel, global head of public-interest litigation: Aye

M. Jacques Yves-Laurent DE RUILLE, III, Director: Oui, Oui

Dr. Sophie Selbsteiger Morchekarang, M.D., Ph.D., Director, global head of transformational medical grants, interim President of the McKay Center of Oncology, co-President and Chief Research Officer of the Norman "Trey" Selbsteiger, III Center for Immunodeficiency Research: Aye

Mr. Norman Selbsteiger, IV, Chairman: Aye

A round of applause. The motion had passed with unanimous assent.

Rust had a noble future.

Acknowledgements

A pseudonymous work regrettably must be coy in its acknowledgements, but no labor is ever undertaken alone. I have received invaluable feedback and criticism from friends, family, and editors, and the work is better for it.

They know who they are, and to them I say: Thank You.

About Ferrox Fiction

Ferrox Fiction (www.ferroxfiction.com) is an experimental imprint seeking to fill a particular niche: novella-length fiction in and about business-oriented topics. To restate that goal immodestly, it is to create and establish said niche, which as best we can tell is heretofore nearly nonexistent. *The Parable of Rust* is the first of, we hope, more works in this genre. Inquiries can be sent to editor@ferroxfiction.com.

A pseudonymous work is dependent to an unusual degree on word of mouth for marketing. If you, dear reader, enjoyed this novella, please say so to your friends, on social media, and in the ratings sections of online retailers.

Amos welcomes all comments, criticism, raves, and lambasts, which can be sent to amos@ferroxfiction.com. He may or may not respond but will read them all.

Made in the USA
Middletown, DE
16 September 2023